For Jonathan

Cassie's Magic Flowers

The Story of Calico Crossings™

Written by Nan Roloff

Illustrated by Nancy Duell

There was once a little girl by the name of Cassie. She was very much like other little girls—she loved to play with her friends, hardly ever cleaned her room, and had a little brother who followed her everywhere.

But Cassie wasn't exactly like other little girls—and this is why. She lived in a town that you can't find on any map—a strange little town where everything was black and white. That was just the way things were.

Each new day looked exactly like the one before it. It was never winter, spring, summer or fall in the town, but somewhere in between. Nothing ever changed. And nobody ever asked why or how the town got to be that way—no one except Cassie.

Every day Cassie would wake up, look out her window and think, "Today will be different—I just know it will. Today something exciting will happen." Cassie was so bored with the way things were.

One evening, after her little brother Corky was tucked into bed, Cassie sat down on her porch and gazed over the black and white roofs of the little town. Stretching out under the rising moon were rows upon rows of little houses that all looked the same.

"I'm so bored," Cassie said to herself. "Surely somewhere things are different than they are here. They just *have* to be!"

The first bright star of the night twinkled overhead.

"Star light, star bright—
The first star I see tonight,
I wish I may, I wish I might
Have the wish I wish tonight."

Cassie closed her eyes and wished with all her heart. Suddenly the star shot across the sky, blazing a brilliant trail behind it unlike anything Cassie had ever seen. It was a stream of color, lighting up the sky.

"Thump." The star seemed to land right in Cassie's own backyard. She was sure it was all a dream!

The next morning, Cassie told Corky about it. "It was so beautiful. I must have imagined it."

But Corky wouldn't hear of that! Sure, he got bored, too. And he would daydream sometimes. But he knew that whenever he got really bored, he could count on Cassie. She was always there, making funny faces or standing on her head to make him laugh. She was a dreamer all right, but she didn't see things that weren't there! He grabbed her skirt and tried to pull her out to the backyard.

"Okay, Corky! Maybe it really did happen! You never know!"

Sure enough, there in the soft, gray grass was the spot where the bright, burning star had landed and disappeared into the earth. Behind it, the star had left several little seeds in bright beautiful colors.

"Corky! It really *did* happen! What kind of seeds do you think they are?" Corky pointed to Cassie's watering can.

"Right! Let's plant them and see. I just know they have to be something wonderful!"

As Corky dragged over Cassie's watering can, Cassie got down on her knees and dug into the soft, gray earth. What did she care if she ended up smudged from head to toe? Carefully, she poked holes with her fingers and tenderly pushed the little seeds into the ground. With the first sprinkle from her watering can, sprouts immediately pushed their way to the surface and burst into the largest, most beautiful flowers either Cassie or Corky had ever seen. They weren't black or white—but strange, exciting new colors in patterns of gingham, dots and calico! Each flower had a heart in its center.

"Corky, look . . . I just knew things could be better!"

With that, Cassie reached over to the flower she thought was most beautiful. It leaned towards her invitingly with a fragrance so wonderful she couldn't resist picking it.

And do you know what happened? Cassie turned calico from head to toe. That's because this was not just an ordinary flower. If picked by the right person, it could cast wonderful spells. Because Cassie was always optimistic about things turning better, the flower was magic in her hands. For these flowers could tell whose heart was in the right place, and whose wasn't.

Corky couldn't have been happier if it had happened to him and was jumping up and down and dancing all around.

"Here Corky, this one's for you. That's for believing me."

As soon as Cassie handed Corky the blue flower, his bonnet began to turn until he was in blue down to his booties. For the flower knew that Corky had a faithful heart. Around their feet the grass began turning green, and calico flowers began to spring from the ground.

Cassie and Corky ran around touching everything in sight, laughing with delight at the bright colors and patterns that appeared, but the colors stopped right at Cassie's gate and would go no further.

Word of the magic flowers spread throughout the black and white town. The other citizens of the town gathered in front of the Dry Goods Store to talk about the strange occurrence. Some were jealous of Cassie and said unkind things, while others said they thought the colors were ugly.

"Who does she think she is," said Mr. Chintz the banker ". . . wanting things to be different."

"Yeah—what's the matter with the way things are?" said Mr. Bolt of the Dry Goods Store.

"I suppose she thinks she's somebody special now," humphed Millie Mae Picot.

"It's black magic, if you ask me," said Poppy Lynn. "I'm keeping my distance from her!"

Everyone agreed not to invite Cassie to any of their parties or to speak to her . . . everyone except Dotty Swiss and her little sister, Pokey Dot.

"Well!" said Dotty with a stamp of her foot. "I think you're all just nasty and horrible to talk about Cassie that way!"

"I refuse to be seen with anyone who looks as ridiculous as she does," sniffed Millie Mae.

"I think she looks just fine, and if you ask me, you're just jealous because the star fell in her yard and not yours!"

"Well . . . I never!"

"Cassie has always been a good friend to all of us. And now, just because she's different, you won't have anything to do with her!" scolded Dotty. "You ought to be ashamed!"

Pokey Dot was thinking over the situation very slowly and carefully. As she saw it, Cassie had always been nice to her, so shouldn't she be nice back? Wasn't it as simple as that? Did all this other stuff about colors really matter? She didn't understand why everyone was so upset. Neither did her pet, Mr. Turtle, who pulled his head into his shell as the arguing grew louder.

"Come, Pokey Dot. I can see we aren't wanted here," said Dotty Swiss as she took Pokey's hand and stomped away from the gathering in front of the Dry Goods Store.

Mayor Carruthers sat listening with an interested look on his face. He had seen the colorful house off in the distance and was fascinated. So what if what had happened to Cassie made her different. Different wasn't always bad, was it? Shouldn't they look into it first before making up their minds? The more he heard about the magic flowers, the more he felt sure they must be—to put it in Carruthers' own words—"stupendillious, ultra-beauteous and terrifical!"

Hiding under the Dry Goods Store porch was Calico Kitty. No one had ever actually seen Kitty, but she was famous throughout the town. You see, Kitty was always sneaking into the kitchens of others and cooking wonderful things. The problem was she never bothered to clean up—so she wasn't always welcome. Calico Kitty loved beautiful things, even if she was messy herself. They made her purr with pleasure. And these magic flowers sounded just like the kind of thing she would like to see, so she immediately began to creep from porch to alley to roof to Cassie's house.

In the distance, Ricky Rack was trying to listen in on the conversation. He lived in a treehouse out in the forest and never spoke to anyone during his rare trips into town. In fact, he had no friends at all. He didn't need any, he said to himself. He was perfectly able to take care of himself. Ricky Rack didn't need *anybody!*

He thought everyone was stupid for even caring about the magic flowers. There was no such thing as magic or wishes coming true. *He* knew! He had certainly made enough wishes—and not a thing had happened. Somebody said maybe the star had fallen in Cassie's yard because she was always doing nice things for others. Well, look at the way everyone was turning on her now! Being nice to others was a waste of time as far as he was concerned. But still, he wondered what the colors really looked like.

Dotty huffed and puffed up the walk to her neat little house with Pokey in tow. The freshly-starched lace curtains fluttered and the china rattled in the cupboard as she slammed the door behind her.

"Now you get ready to go for a walk Pokey, and don't you dawdle. I'm going to take Cassie a pot of my special spiced tea, and I don't want it to get cold before we get there. If the rest of the town doesn't like it, it's just too bad!"

Dotty mixed her special tea in her neat little pot, and off they went to Cassie's house. Cassie welcomed them at the door.

"Oh, I was hoping you would come," Cassie said as she gave Dotty and Pokey a big hug. "I don't know what everyone is so afraid of."

"Well, phooey on them. They're just jealous!"

There was another knock at the door. Cassie opened it to find Mayor Carruthers—what a surprise!

"Aren't you afraid of what everyone else will think of you?" Cassie asked.

"Poppycock, my endearious one! I don't see why I should let those sillybillies stand in the way of my mental enrichment. Who knows, maybe these flowers will be of magnabenefit to the world!"

They all went out into Cassie's bright yard to see the flowers. Meanwhile, Ricky Rack had sneaked to the edge of Cassie's yard and was watching everything through the fence. Just a few feet away, Calico Kitty sat watching, too.

"Oh—they're simply beautiful," said Dotty.

"Go ahead . . . pick one . . . they don't wither," said Cassie.

A stately lavender flower leaned toward Dotty, and she reached out to pick it. As soon as it was in her hand, she turned lavender and purple.

"Oh, I feel just wonderful!" smiled Dotty. The flower knew that Dotty was loyal and true. It was meant for her alone.

A little purple and red flower brushed against Pokey as if to say "pick me." This flower knew what an honest, sensible little girl Pokey was. It belonged to Pokey because she always saw things just as they were. As soon as she picked it, she and Mr. Turtle changed, too.

Ricky Rack could hardly believe his eyes! By now Calico Kitty was purring so loudly she was afraid the others would discover her in her hiding place.

A tall flower with a green heart in its center tapped Carruthers on the shoulder. It belonged to Carruthers because he valued knowledge and truth. When he picked it, he turned green! "Fantasticular!" he cried.

As soon as everyone had gone back into Cassie's house for tea, Ricky Rack started to creep out of his hiding place, but a rustle nearby stopped him in his tracks. Out crept Calico Kitty, up to a beautiful yellow flower. She purred and purred as she rubbed up against the flower, and it seemed to pet her in return. Suddenly Kitty picked the flower and turned a beautiful shade of sunshine yellow, for the flower knew how very much Calico Kitty loved beauty. "Meow-wow-wow," said Kitty contentedly.

After Kitty left, Ricky Rack sneaked into Cassie's yard and looked at the flowers. A blue and red one seemed to be leaning toward him, then it would sway away, as though it couldn't make up its mind.

"I think this is some silly trick," he said. "Let's see if it works every time." With that, Ricky Rack yanked the red and blue flower from the ground. But instead of Ricky turning red and blue, the flower faded to black and white.

"Just as I thought . . . it's all phoney." Ricky was going to throw the flower down on the ground and stomp on it, but for some reason he stopped. Carefully, he tucked the flower under his cap, then crawled through the fence and went back home to his tree-house in the forest.

As for Dotty, Pokey, Carruthers and Kitty, they each left a trail of color as they walked home. The streets leading from Cassie's house to theirs were transformed, as well as their houses! Even the porch Kitty curled up under turned a warm, sunny yellow.

As soon as the rest of the town saw what had happened to Dotty and Pokey and the Mayor, they began to soften. Maybe this change was a good thing. Maybe Cassie was okay after all. Maybe the colors could happen to them, too!

Little by little, everyone began to stop being quite as afraid and wanted to know more—everyone but Ricky Rack. Ricky Rack sat in his treehouse in the black and white forest and laughed at them all. What fools they were to believe in such a silly thing. He knew better. He took the flower from under his cap—scoffed, then stuck it back. As he folded his arms across his chest with a scowl, he thought he heard a low moan below . . . and then another.

"What's that? Humph—just my imagination," Ricky said to himself.

"H-o-w-l!"

"Hmm—maybe I better go check this out." Ricky climbed down his ladder and looked around. There in the bushes he saw what looked like a tattered paw.

It was a dog, and he was old and tired and all beat up. He looked up at Ricky with big, sad eyes.

"Go away! You can't stay here! Sho-o-o!" Ricky said.

The dog nuzzled Ricky's hand, and his tail wagged, making a soft "thump, thump" sound on the ground.

"Oh, no you don't. I don't want anybody hanging around my house, eating my food and sleeping in my bed."

Still the dog stared at Ricky. He tried to get up but was too weak and hungry. Perhaps he had been someone's faithful friend for years and then been abandoned in favor of a younger pet. Ricky felt a slight stirring of pity.

"Well . . . maybe you can stay a day or two. But only till you're better! Then you have to leave!"

The dog licked his hand. Suddenly, Ricky wasn't so sure he wanted the dog to leave. Gently he put the dog on his back and carried him piggyback up into the treehouse.

He laid the dog in his bed and tucked a blanket around him. Then, for no reason really, he went to his cupboard and got out the piece of chocolate he had been saving for himself for a special occasion.

"Here," he said handing it to the dog. "You take it. You need it more than I do."

Ricky quietly watched as the dog nibbled the chocolate from his hand. "Maybe I could call you Gus," he said. Suddenly, bright red and blue petals peeked out from under Ricky's cap as he stroked the dog's head. As the dog licked Ricky's face, Ricky began to change color until he was red and blue all over, but he didn't even notice until the dog began to change color, too. All around Ricky the treehouse began to take on new colors and patterns. For Ricky's flower bloomed just as friendships bloom and grow.

Ricky Rack grabbed his new friend and ran to the window to watch as the trees in the forest began to change, from the lowest root to the highest leaf. Before he knew it, the entire forest was filled with patches of bright calico. His heart welled up with happiness to see the beautiful sight, and what made it even better was having someone to share it with.

The citizens of the town saw the forest change, too, and they knew that Ricky Rack, the boy who never spoke to any of them, had been touched by the flowers. Then everyone in the town, some alone and some in groups, went to Cassie's house to see the flowers. Soon they all had opened their hearts to the magic Cassie's hope had brought to them.

Once that happened, people began to smile and tip their hats at each other on the streets. Color swept across the town and the hillside, making the fields look like squares in a colorful patchwork quilt. After that day, the town became known as Calico Crossings. Cassie was called Calico Cassie, because it was she who had proven things can be better if you just believe they can.

The End